This book should be returned to any branch of the
Lancashire County Library on or before the date shown

Lancashire County Library,
County Hall Complex,
1st floor Christ Church Precinct,
Preston, PR1 8XJ

Lancashire
County
Council

www.lancashire.gov.uk/libraries

LL1(A)

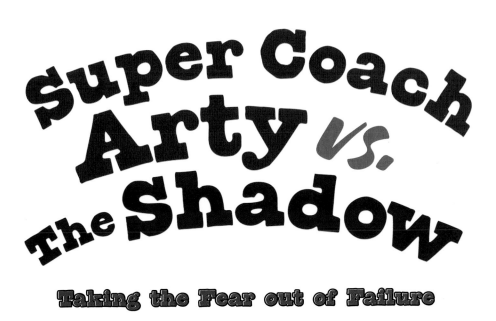

Super Coach Arty vs. The Shadow

Taking the Fear out of Failure

Lorraine Thomas
Illustrated by Simon Greaves
Digitally coloured by Phill Evans

Jessica Kingsley Publishers
London and Philadelphia

First published in 2018
by Jessica Kingsley Publishers
73 Collier Street
London N1 9BE, UK
and
400 Market Street, Suite 400
Philadelphia, PA 19106, USA

www.jkp.com

Library of Congress Cataloging in Publication Data
A CIP catalog record for this book is available from the Library of Congress

British Library Cataloguing in Publication Data
A CIP catalogue record for this book is available from the British Library

ISBN 978 1 78592 441 5
eISBN 978 1 78450 815 9

Printed and bound in China

For Harry

"A life lived in love means you cannot fail."

Harry Corder Greaves

Acknowledgements

I love you Jerry, Holly, Josh and Ben. Thank you for welcoming Arty into our family. You are the very best team I could ever wish for, and thanks to you I am making this dream come true.

Simon, you are a brilliant, creative and inspirational artist. You are a true friend. Your strength and humour have kept me going in the maze. Thank you, Phill, for bringing Simon's wonderful illustrations to life in such a colourful, vibrant and imaginative way.

Gill, Elaine, Sarah, Tree, Tom T, Tom S, Kate, Becky, Matt, Bernadette, Iara, Nancy and Leonora – thanks for joining "Team Arty" and sharing your time, energy, enthusiasm, professional expertise and fantastic ideas.

I am indebted to Claire Purcell and everyone at Dulwich Hamlet Junior School who has made Arty possible.

With a very special thank you to Joshua, Jason, Anna, Leonora, Mimmo, Hettie, Alexei, Rocco, Freya, Ava Mae, Nancy H, Adam, Nancy R, Greta and Emily who are sharing their own Super Coach drawings with us in this book.

With thanks to all the children it has been my privilege to coach over the years. You have all taught me so much. This book is packed full of your brilliant and practical ideas. You are the real experts. You have all played an important part in the creative process and helped Arty to develop and grow.

Super Coach Arty is only here because of my editor, James Cherry at Jessica Kingsley Publishers. Thanks for your vision, James, and for believing in Arty. It's been good fun working with you and I appreciate the support, advice and expertise that you have given me at every step of our journey.

My life changed forever today.

Have you noticed how often adults lose the plot and behave in an unreasonable way? Take my mum. I love her, but she can be difficult. It's Monday morning and, with no warning, she comes crashing into my dreams firing instructions. She repeats herself. And she's speaking so quickly it's like she's pressed her own fast-forward button.

"Come on. Time to get up. Only forty-five minutes before we have to leave." She needs to relax. A whole forty-five minutes! Parents have weird ideas about time. Always rushing and planning. No wonder they're stressed.

Mum's also developed this habit of asking me questions and then answering them herself. Here she goes!

"Do you know where your PE kit is? You need to be in early for basketball practice. No, of course you don't. I'll have to find it."

"What do you want for breakfast? You've got that big maths test today. You'd better have something. Are you worried about the test? There's nothing to worry about. Just make sure you don't panic."

Well, when an adult tells you not to worry, you know it IS time to panic! I'm rubbish at maths. I know Mum is trying to make me feel better, but she's only making it worse. My heart sinks.

It's not just maths. Whenever I get asked a question in class the same thing happens. My mind turns to mush and my body turns to jelly. Even if I know the answer — it's locked inside me.

The day stretches ahead of me like a prison sentence. I could really do with some help to get me through this one.

I can help. I hear a quiet whisper. Asking for help is the first step.

Oh no. Now I'm hearing strange noises. It's going to be one of those days.

I'm your Super Coach. I'm inside your head. Only you can hear me.

What are you talking about? What kind of coach? A sports coach?

Sort of. But the game I'm coaching you for is your life. My team rules are simple: make a difference, achieve your personal best — and have fun, of course.

How do I know you are real?

Make your own mind up on that one.

I mean...what do you look like?

Nothing yet. I'm inside your head so you get to decide. Use your imagination. Think about something you enjoy and create me.

Well, playing frisbee is always fun. Love my music, that's a possibility. Or maybe one of my favourite animals? What about a puppy or monkey... or hedgehog?

I'm your Super Coach. You can choose.

I really haven't got time for this...

Hang on, I've got it. I love basketball and drawing. Here we go — I'll call you Super Coach Arty. And here are a couple of pets to keep you company.

Super Coach Arty. I like that.

It's no good, you won't be able to help me. I know I'm going to fail the test this afternoon. Even a Super Coach can't help me succeed. Success is about getting everything right — right?

Wrong! Success is about doing your best. I don't judge your success and failure in terms of a score, a grade or a number on a piece of paper.

Well you're out of touch then. You have no idea how tough it is being me. I'm under pressure all the time to get top marks. My parents will be so disappointed in me if I don't do well. They'll say it doesn't matter, but I know it does. I don't want to let anyone down.

Maybe we can change the way you feel about that. Arty's voice is quiet now.

Shaking my head, I wolf down my toast and dash out of the door. Walking along the road, I hear a booming voice, and I sense a familiar shadow following me.

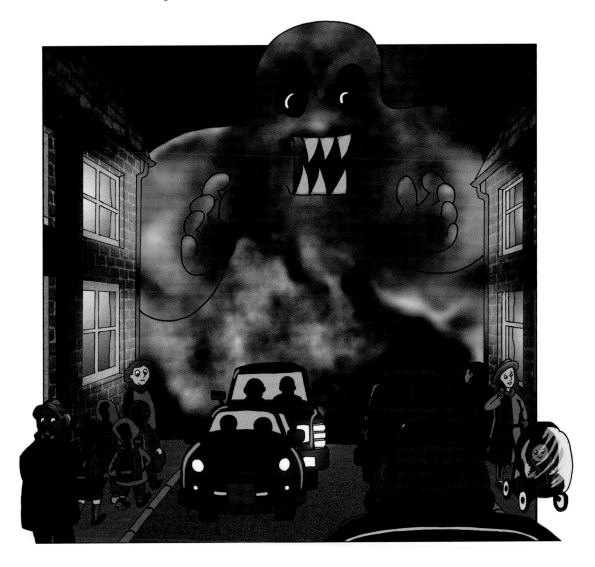

It grows taller as I walk, and my fear vibrates between my ears. "What if I fail badly? What if I get easy questions wrong? They'll laugh at me. How disappointed will Mum and Dad be? I'm so rubbish at maths."

Now listen up. Your fear of failure is common. I can help you with it.

I can just about hear Arty's voice above the racket.

"You're wasting your time, Arty," I reply.

Glad you mentioned time. Whenever you feel stressed today, I'll say **"time out."** But you must concentrate to hear me.

What good will that do?

My "time out" will remind you that you always have choices, even when stuff that you don't like happens. It will give you time and space to decide how you want to respond.

Arty's voice is a little louder now.

It's normal to feel worried sometimes. When you do, worry comes charging into your brain like an electric current. Flashing like a huge electronic scoreboard in your head. It's very powerful because the "emotional" part of your brain that influences how you feel is well developed. It's been in full working order since you were very small. Those painful feelings are shouting at full volume, like a giant crowd of children.

I guess you're right, Arty. When I'm worried the feeling gets bigger and bigger. Louder and louder. It takes over my head.

Yes, that's why it can seem overwhelming. And when you worry, chemicals are released inside your brain. They clog everything up and it stops working.

So that's why I can't think straight.

Exactly. Even a small problem can seem huge. But once you start to relax, the chemicals clear. Then you can begin to think clearly again.

When you worry or feel anxious, that chemical reaction in your brain means that you literally blow your top. It's like sending me, your Super Coach, into outer space. You lose your connection with me and you listen only to your emotions and feelings.

So, let me get this clear, when I hear "time out" I have to try to get back in touch with you Arty, and then you can help me?

Yes. Think of it like this: A... B... C...

Arty's voice is very powerful.

A... Accept how you feel. Give your feeling a name. "Name it and tame it."

I'm going to call it Fear then. It's not just inside my head. I can see it too. It's like a shadow following me. I shudder as I say it.

B... Breathe... Breathe... Breathe.

Obviously, I do that anyway. Otherwise I'd be dead!

Take a deep breath in. As though you are smelling your favourite soup.

Come off it, Arty. More like favourite **pizza**. Pepperoni!

As you breathe out — slowly — imagine that you are blowing away any tension that you feel. You are blowing away Fear — and making room for me.

And C... Connect with your coach — that's me, of course. Every time you take a deep breath in, your connection with me grows stronger. I need oxygen too. Picture me. Ask yourself, what would Super Coach Arty say?

Your feelings are well developed already and come across LOUDLY! But I'm still young, still developing. My voice is much quieter so you must listen carefully to hear what I am saying. But I am always here.

OK. But it won't do any good.

If you think you can, you probably will. If you think you can't, you'll be right.

No idea what you are talking about. You're losing the plot Arty. I thought you might have been able to help me but you're wasting my time. I'm going to be late for basketball and I should have been practising my times tables for my test.

I can't hear a reply. The dreadful voice inside my head is drowning Arty out. I try hard to concentrate and remember my times tables, but now my little monster brother is shouting. "Look! Look! I can get to school before you!"

As he races off on his scooter at full speed, my life flashes before me. I can only begin to imagine what Mum will say if he hurts himself. He's speeding down the steep hill towards the busy road. I run as though my life depends on it and just manage to grab him as he crashes into the loud group of children at the bottom, scattering them like angry ants.

Sammy turns around and frowns at me. I hear the word, "Idiot." My life is going to be a misery in class today.

I glance out of the corner of my eye. I'm hoping that at least by sprinting, I've left The Shadow behind. Great, it's gone.

But then I see it's holding the school gate open for me. It's raining so, after all that, basketball practice is delayed until lunchtime. It's only now I realise I've left my English homework on the kitchen table. That means trouble with Mr Tinns.

The playground is full of jostling children and so much noise. My brother's friends are screaming. I can't hear myself think.

Time out! Accept, Breathe and Connect with me.

I can just make out Arty's soft tone trying hard to be heard above the racket.

Think of your brain in two parts. I'm up here and down below is where all your feelings live. It's just like this playground full of noisy children. All your feelings are trying to be the loudest, all wanting to be heard above the rest.

Yes, that sounds like our playground all right!

Here they are.

No wonder they argue, Arty. Some are much better than others.

They're all different, just like you and your brother. It isn't a case of good and bad, they all play an important part in your life.

But I can only hear one voice, yelling above the rest. Fear is shouting. It's getting louder. It's winning. Fear's Shadow is threatening me. I just want it to go away.

OK, let's think about that shadow in a different way. Arty is whispering. What's it like?

Fear is towering over me.

Now, can you make it seem smaller? Less powerful? Less in control of you?

You don't want much! OK, I think I have an idea. I will imagine it's a balloon, full of air. I'm going to try to pop it with my pencil... But I can't. It's too strong, Arty. This is hopeless.

That didn't work. That's helpful because now we know we must try something else. I am hearing Arty loud and clear now. If we give up, The Shadow wins.

Let's try letting some of the air out. Yes, I can do that. It's getting a little bit smaller. It's beginning to shrink, Arty. But only a tiny bit. And the voice isn't quite so loud.

Good. The first step is the most important. We'll keep working on that.

We can work together to make these loud, painful and challenging voices like Fear much quieter. Then you'll be able to hear lots of other voices – the fun and happy ones.

How, Arty?

Look. Every day I'm collecting information about you and filing it carefully on these **special memory sticks**. Like the ones you use on your computer. Arty's hands are full.

Cool sticks. What sort of stuff?

It's your success file. **Arty is smiling.** Take a look... Values, Qualities, Skills and Strengths — Courage, Effort, Attitude, Kindness, Honesty, Problem-solving. Every time you do something that shows one of these, I store the evidence. You can't argue with the evidence. See? You have loads! When those difficult voices like Fear are chattering away, we can use this evidence to challenge what they are saying. To quieten them down when they are getting in the way of us thinking clearly.

What's the voice saying now?

My body tenses as I answer the question. I'm rubbish at times tables.

How true is that? Arty waits patiently.

True, I suppose.

Let's look at the evidence and decide. What times tables do you know?

Well, I suppose I know a few, Arty — 1, 2, 3, 4, 5, 6 and 7. Oh yes, and 0, 10 and 100 because they're easy.

So, you already know lots of your times tables. **Arty grins.** You may not know your 8 times table **YET**, but you will in the future. The evidence shows us that when you work hard, put in lots of effort and practise, you can remember your tables. I think Fear is making it up. Saying things that we can prove are untrue.

Doesn't seem so bad when you say it like that, Super Coach. You're right.

My feelings of joy are only temporary and as soon as I get into the classroom they disappear. My English homework — I don't have it. Now Panic sets in. I can hear it screaming at me and I begin to feel hot and sweaty. "You're in trouble now. You are so disorganised. Mr Tinns is going to be cross and keep you in at lunchtime. You are silly." The screaming gets louder.

Time out! A... B... C... Accept. Breathe. Connect. Think of your choices.

Shall I just hope he doesn't ask for the English homework? He is a bit forgetful. Or come clean and suffer the consequences? I am normally very organised and haven't forgotten it before. Mr Tinns is usually very reasonable. I decide to take the rap.

Good. Arty approves. You're choosing to be honest even though you may be told off.

I notice that I haven't heard that horrible voice for a while.

English class is going OK and I'm quite enjoying it until Mr Tinns says, "What do you think about Macbeth's response here? I want everyone's hand up. There's no 'right' or 'wrong' answer." He's looking directly at me.

The Shadow is suffocating me. That voice is in my head again. It's close. I can hardly move. Everyone looks at me. I'm paralysed. I've got loads of ideas but I can't say them out loud, they just get stuck inside.

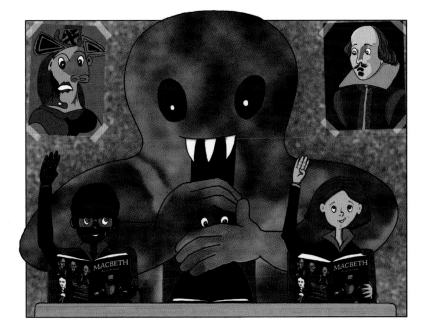

That voice in my head is loud again, but I can just about hear Arty.

Time out! A... B... C...

Accept — I'm embarrassed, but that's OK. It will pass. I can handle it, I think!

Breathe — 1, 2, 3, 4, 5. Deeply. Thinking about my pizza helps. Keep breathing. As I breathe out, I can see The Shadow is billowing in the breeze. I blow it around. Hey, that's quite cool.

Connect with Arty — and choose how to respond. I imagine that, as I put my hand up, I'm taking the top off my big bottle of ideas and letting them all flow out.

Inspired! I can hear Arty clearly now. What does it say on the label?

It says, "I can."

Now Mr Tinns is next to me, waiting for me to talk.

My words come tumbling out and I have no idea what I am saying or if I am making any sense.

He looks at me and smiles. "Well done for having a go. Great idea, very insightful and creative. I like the way you gave us a specific example. I really want you to share your thoughts with the class more often. It will help everybody."

I can only just hear Mr Tinns because Arty is cheering so loudly.

The bell rings and I feel so happy as I walk out into the playground with my friends. We're going to have fun this lunchtime.

I see the new twins, Latif and Nadia, sitting nervously on the bench. They are together, but look very alone.

I suggest to my friends that we ask them to play with us. Sammy gives me a withering look. Suddenly, I realise that The Shadow is back again. It's confronting me. I feel so small. The Shadow gets taller and towers over me.

Sammy's tongue stings like a whip. "Loser!"

That powerful voice rips through my head. It's Fear. Over and over again.

"I'm failing in the playground too." It's repeating itself. "I am so unpopular. They're all laughing at me. I've really blown it. I want to be liked. I need Sammy on my side. All my friends will turn against me."

I do nothing. But instead of feeling OK about this, I feel bad. Even The Shadow is laughing at me.

Time out! A... B... C... It's Arty waving a memory stick with "Kind" on it.
I breathe and try to think straight. Hard in the heat of the moment.
Stick with Sammy? Or do the right thing? Do I want to be the person
Sammy wants me to be, or the person I want to be? I can decide. I try
to stand up straight and focus even though I am crumbling inside. "Let's
put it to a vote? I am definitely in favour. Imagine how you would feel,"
I hear myself saying. It sounds much more confident than I'm feeling
inside. "Who is with me?"

Good. This is your choice. Arty smiles at me and sings. You are being
the person you want to be, not the one other people make you become.
You're imagining how the twins feel. You're being kind and treating other
people well.

Arty gives me the thumbs up. I feel much stronger.

To my surprise the vote goes in my favour. Sammy looks annoyed. The
twins are thrilled to join in. They're great fun. I notice they've left their
nervous shadows sitting silently and sullenly on the bench.

My Shadow collapses and the voice disappears.

Lunchtime is getting better and better. Time for basketball practice now and I rush to get ready. The twins come too. I'm asked to captain our team. Sammy's playing for the opposition. The sides are balanced but we're losing right from the start. Even Ezra, our star player, has his head down. He is so despondent. It's overwhelming and his shadow darkens the court. We may as well give up at this rate.

Time out! Accept... Breathe... Connect with Super Coach.

It's Arty trying to get my attention.

You only fail when you stop trying. Do you want to sit on the bench, letting life happen to you, or do you want to play a real role, taking responsibility and being in the driving seat of your life?

I have to admit that Arty is making a good point — AGAIN!

I focus on my memory sticks, searching desperately for something that will help.

Everything you are looking for is here. Arty helps me focus.

I can motivate a team. That's why I've been chosen to captain it. I'm fast — I really sprinted down the hill this morning. And I can turn situations around — look what happened with Sammy. I have already found ways to begin to shrink my Shadow and quieten Fear. But can I help Ezra reduce the power of his shadow? Yes. I can use my memory sticks to make sure Ezra's emotion doesn't overwhelm us all — and help the whole team.

"Come on everyone. Heads up, we can do this. Believe you can get the next point, Ezra. You have done it so many times before, I know you can do it again."

It's my voice, not Arty's. I'm shouting loudly and confidently.

The ball is way above me. I jump high and pass Ezra the ball. He makes a spectacular layup. High-fives all round. It's a turning point in the game.

I've forgotten about my Shadow.

I can hear lots of loud voices again, but not Fear and Panic — I hardly recognise them, they've been drowned out all day. Now I am hearing new voices — Joy and Excitement.

The bell rings and my happiness evaporates. The moment I am dreading arrives. Mr Tinns hands out the test. My Shadow surrounds me.

My heart is pounding as I open the paper. The first question is division, my worst nightmare! Bound to fail. Stress is building up inside me like an erupting volcano. It's a monster inside my head. It's growing. It's playing with my brain. It's eating Arty. I can't think.

I scan the classroom. It's full. How come everyone else seems fine? I feel very alone. This question is impossible.

So, let's look at this a different way.

It's Arty. He's surviving. Just.

Even the word "IMPOSSIBLE" says "I'M POSSIBLE."

Remember our ABC... Accept how you feel. Trying to understand why you feel a certain way can help you. It's the first step to managing the feeling instead of letting it have control over you.

But everyone here looks so calm. I'm trying not to worry, but it isn't working. I need Arty to understand it's not that easy for me. Why am I the only one who can't do this?

What you are feeling is totally normal.

Me — normal? That's good news, Arty...if you're right!

Look at what is happening inside your head now. Processing negatives is hard. So when you tell yourself not to worry, you just worry more... worry... Worry... WORRY.

Worry Worry worry Worry WORRY WORRY worry WORRY worry worry WORRY Worry WORRY

If you know so much, Arty, tell me what I should do. I have no idea and you seem to have all the answers.

You do too. Tell yourself how you **do** want to feel instead of how you **don't** want to feel. Be positive. Your brain gets positive messages loud and clear.

You mean like setting the GPS in our car. I need to know my destination otherwise I'll never get there.

Exactly.

Come off it, Arty. Get real. Obviously I'd like to feel calm. But how can I even begin to relax at a time like this?

Try turning that division sign into something that will help you. A picture that makes you smile instead of frightens you.

I'm transforming it from a symbol of evil into a smiley face — two eyes and a mouth.

I can see Arty is fascinated as my pencil talks to the paper.

Now I'm going to draw a circle round it and pretend it's a ball — and up it goes into the basketball hoop. Slam dunk! I feel a lot better.

Very creative. Arty is applauding. You're getting the hang of this!

Good. Another important success. Your memory stick is filling up.

But how can the memory stick help me with the test?

It's proof that you've already got lots of skills, strengths and qualities to help you when you face a challenge. Like this test. What did you do when you were under pressure because you'd forgotten your homework?

Came clean.

You were honest and took responsibility — even though you knew it could mean trouble. What happened at basketball practice when your team was losing?

Tried my hardest.

Exactly. You were a great role model. You were positive and kept going even when it was tough. You motivated your team.

And when you had to deal with Sammy in the playground?

I took a deep breath and kept calm because I knew it was important to be kind.

That took a great deal of courage. So there is the evidence that you can keep calm, focus, be courageous and give it all you've got — even when you're under a lot of pressure. You have all these strengths. Forget masks and capes — these are the qualities of a real "superhero." Use them now.

My own super powers. Now you're talking, Arty. But I'm still rubbish at maths.

What happens if I try this question and get it wrong?

Having a go is the most important thing.

I am not going to be able to move Arty on this one.

You're saying I don't have to do everything perfectly, Arty, as long as I do my best?

Absolutely. Your personal best is much more important than perfection. Just give it a try.

There will always be stuff in life that you find hard. But you can choose how you handle it. You always have choices. When you take the ball on the court, you have choices about your next move. The same here.

You mean I must do the test, Arty, but I don't have to start with this question. I can go to one that I can do and try this again later. This one about time looks easy.

Yes, there are always choices. Get off the bench and take action!

Arty is pointing a determined finger.

Your score in a maths test doesn't tell me anything about you as a person and that's what's most important.

The classroom melts away and I'm back in my favourite happy place — the basketball court. Arty opens my "success" memory stick. It's packed.

 Loving your family...even when the behaviour of your mum and brother is very irritating.

Doing what you believe is right...even if it means standing up to your friends.

Taking responsibility...owning up even when it gets you into trouble.

 Respecting other people's views...even when you disagree.

Being positive...looking for solutions even when they are difficult to find.

Trying your hardest...keeping going and not giving up.

Asking for help...a sign of great strength.

Treating other people well and being a kind...making a difference.

I realise that I'm not alone. The crowd are up on their feet, cheering me, calling my name. They're so proud of me. So many familiar faces. It's so loud, but I can still hear Arty very clearly.

Keep perspective — the big picture. Remember your family and friends love you. That love isn't based on any score. Whatever you get in your test, they will always love you.

I hadn't thought of it like that, thanks Arty.

I answer the question about time. I'm good at that. And I manage most of the questions about area. Some of the subjects are very difficult, but I try my hardest. Sometimes I can feel The Shadow coming back. When I begin to hear its voice, I connect with Arty and take a good look at my success memory stick.

Does everyone have a coach?

Every person has their own unique Super Coach.

And as well as you, there are always lots of people I can talk to and ask for help — Mum, Dad, my friends, my teacher, my sports coach.

Yes. But remember, don't just talk about the problem…

Stop there — I know! I need to have a strategy. Just like in our matches. Think about what I can do to take a step towards the solution — something practical that's inside my control. Think choices. Like asking Ezra to explain division to me — he's a whizz at maths.

Great idea.

I'm beginning to sound like you now!

I notice something is changing. The air is hissing out of the balloon and that tall Shadow fizzles and shrinks as it disappears into the sky.

The test is over. No idea how I've done, but it doesn't seem to matter so much anymore because I know I've done my best. I feel good. I'm letting my Shadow go. The scary voice inside my head is totally silent.

Will you always be there for me, Arty?

Yes. We're a team. You created me. You have all the answers inside you. Just ask.

I smile. It's taken me all day but now I realise why Arty's voice is so familiar.

It belongs to me. It's mine. Arty was my voice all along.

Activities for Children

Creating Your Own Super Coach

We can all create our own, special Super Coach.

It's good fun being me. I love to see all the different coaches that children draw. Look, here are some of them.

What do you think the pictures tell us about the children who have drawn them?

Your turn now. Imagine what your Super Coach looks like.

Begin by thinking about all the things you love to do or play with or see or hear or smell or eat. Choose your favourite. Something that will make you smile when you think about it. Have a go at drawing it.

Your Super Coach can be as simple or as complicated as you want it to be. It's your Super Coach. You're creating it.

Now, how about names? What would you like to call your Super Coach?

Remember to Use Your A... B... C...

I love basketball, so I'm always saying "Time out." It's a reminder to press the pause button for a moment and remember **A... B... C...** **A**ccept how I feel, **B**reathe out any stress or tension and **C**onnect with Coach.

What would you like your Super Coach to say to remind you to press the pause button and try the A... B... C...?

Say it out loud!

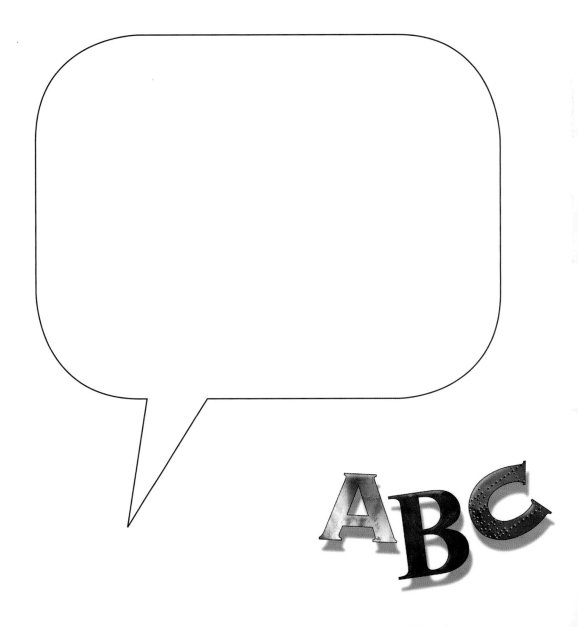

Gathering Evidence for Your Memory Sticks

Now you've read my story, you know just how important those memory sticks are. Every day, you gather new evidence about yourself. When you are worried or frightened, use the evidence to focus on the strengths, skills and qualities you possess. This will help you rise to any challenge.

Here's my challenge for you. How about you start right now?

Think of three things that can be included on your "Success" memory stick. Try to give a specific example for each one. Remember how I define success — loving your family, doing what you believe is right, taking responsibility, respecting other people's views, being positive, trying your hardest, asking for help and treating other people well — making a difference.

Great. Now you have started and can add to the list whenever you want to. It will grow!

What do you think other people who are important in your life would add to your list? How about you ask them and find out?

Arty's Top Tips

My voice can sometimes seem very quiet and it's hard to hear me. But there are lots of things you can do to help you hear your Super Coach, your resilient self. It's just like preparing for a big game.

1. Get a good night's sleep. Your form suffers if you are tired.
2. Leave your devices in the kitchen when you go to bed. They disturb your sleep and mean your brain doesn't have a proper chance to rest. This is very important if you are going to have lots of energy for the adventures you'll face each day.
3. Eat well. Your Super Coach is growing. It's not just about exercising your brain. You must also feed it the right healthy foods.
4. Get lots of exercise so that you feel positive, fit and healthy.
5. Have fun — of course!

These will really help.

Which of the five ideas on the list are you best at doing? Well done, keep it up! Now choose one of the others to focus on over the next seven days. Set yourself a goal — and make it happen.

Thinking Differently about "Fear of Failure"

Now about that "Fear of Failure" Shadow... I feel a bit sorry for it. I know it can seem scary, but I also think it gets a hard time. It comes in useful in so many ways. It's really helped me to grow. I wouldn't be who I am without it.

- ✓ It motivates me to get better.
- ✓ I grow much stronger every time I overcome a challenge it presents.
- ✓ I learn more from the things I haven't been able to do at first than the ones I can do easily.
- ✓ It helps me understand what works and what doesn't. If something doesn't go according to plan, I know it's a good idea to try something different.
- ✓ It's teaching me how to find solutions and solve problems.
- ✓ It's teaching me patience, determination and resilience.
- ✓ Now I know what it's like to be frightened, frustrated, worried and disappointed, it means I can help other people who feel like that too.

How can you turn this Shadow into something that makes you smile?

Note to Parents and Carers from Lorraine

As a parent or carer you will always be a pioneer.

Resilience grows and develops. Every day is an opportunity to make a difference to children, to their view of the world and the way they regard themselves.

Helping children connect with their own Super Coach will empower them and strengthen their confident, resilient self. You are helping them to understand how the brain affects the way they feel. It will put them in the driving seat of their own lives – looking forward to the adventures, rising to challenges and growing stronger through them.

We can raise our own generation of superheroes. Not the superhero who wears a mask and a cape. Our children are real superheroes. We can nurture in our little ones the super powers that will make a difference in our world – compassion, responsibility, empathy, honesty, integrity and love.

The world we leave to our children depends on the children we leave in the world.

Have fun and enjoy the adventure.

Nurturing Resilient Children: Top 10 Tips for Parents and Carers

Here are my top 10 tips for you to use. On the following pages there are practical ways in which you can put them into action. Every time you do this, you will be nurturing resilience, helping children rise to challenges and grow stronger through them.

Every day is an opportunity to make a difference. Each day this week, choose one of the tips from the list below and focus on it for 24 hours. It may be something you are doing well already – do more of it. Or it may be something that you aren't doing now but would like to. These tips are to help you build on your expertise as a parent or carer. You'll have lots of your own great ideas, so make sure you use those too.

1. Be a great resilience role model and children will learn to be resilient too.
2. Make sure you are all getting your five-a-day (sleep, exercise, healthy diet, fun and love).
3. Learn to relax with A... B... C... Accept... Breathe... Connect with your coach and choose an action inside your control.
4. Help children manage their whole range of emotions in a positive way, for example managing stress with healthy habits.
5. Be clear about your family or classroom "success ethos" and focus on children's ACE (Attitude, Commitment and Effort).
6. Challenge self-limiting beliefs and quieten a child's inner critic with specific, evidence-based feedback.
7. Put children in the driving seat with choice and responsibility.
8. Build on strengths to weaken weaknesses – focus on the values, skills, strengths and qualities they have to help them rise to challenges.
9. Press the "pause" button and build reflection skills – if it works, do it again; if it doesn't, do something differently.
10. Think "connection" not "perfection" and "live in the moment." You can't be 100% Mum, Dad or carer all the time. But you can be 100% some of the time. These times are vital. Engage all your senses and focus totally on your children.

1. Be a great resilience role model and children will learn to be resilient too

You will always be a powerful role model and every day is an opportunity to make a difference in children's lives. The more you manage your range of emotions and rise to challenges with practical actions inside your control, the more children will too.

Tips

Look at the list below. These behaviours indicate healthy levels of resilience. Which one are you best at? Choose one to focus on over the next 24 hours. It may be one you are doing well already, or one you want to make some positive changes to.

- ▸ Embrace challenges as opportunities and talk about how you are going to handle them with actions inside your control.
- ▸ Be positive, optimistic and energised – smile more often than you frown and say "yes" more often than "no."
- ▸ Manage stress with healthy habits – go for a walk or swim, have a relaxing bath or book a zumba or yoga class.
- ▸ Work at "responding" rather than "reacting." Take a deep breath and keep calm so that you can be the parent or carer you want to be.
- ▸ Have a positive attitude to "failure" or things not turning out as planned and focus on what you can learn from them.
- ▸ Demonstrate that asking for help is a sign of strength – get them to show you how to do something that they are better at than you.

2. Make sure you are all getting your five-a-day

When you are looking after yourself, you are looking after everyone else. You are the engine room. It's important for all of us to get our five-a-day – sleep, exercise, healthy diet, fun and love. When we are feeling relaxed, healthy and positive, we all find it easier to deal with the challenges of daily life. Take the opportunity to reflect on how you are looking after yourself, and show children that you are working at these things too.

Tips

- ▸ Take five minutes to MOT your five-a-day (sleep, exercise, diet, fun and love). Which one is going best for you now (remember it doesn't have to be perfect!)? Which one would you most like to focus on over the next 24 hours? What can you do that is practical and inside your control to help you?
- ▸ Adults are often telling children that they're spending too long on their screens, for example, but how about creating a boundary for yourself today? Making sure that you have at least one hour of "screen-free" time before bed will give you the chance to relax, and

leaving all devices outside of your bedroom will give you a better quality of sleep.

▶ Before you close your eyes, focus on one thing that has gone well during the day and slip off to sleep with positive thoughts instead of everything that is on your "to-do" list for tomorrow!

3. Learn to relax with A... B... C...
Accept... Breathe... Connect with your coach

A... Accept how they feel

Tips

▶ "Name it and tame it." Giving a feeling a name is often the first step in helping children to believe that they can understand and manage it rather than fight against it.

▶ Avoid saying, "There is nothing to worry about." It is important that children know they can talk to you about how they feel.

▶ Children find negatives hard to process, so help them get into the habit of focusing on how they want to feel instead of how they don't want to feel – relaxed instead of worried, energised instead of tired. Make sure you get into the habit of doing this yourself too.

B... Breathe... Breathe... Breathe

Tips

▶ Play breathing games with your child to help them to learn how to relax. Ask them to focus on their breathing as you count. Encourage them to take a deep breath in through their nose (think of smelling pizza!) and then breathe out any tension in their body.

▶ Get them to try to wriggle each one of their toes in turn as they breathe. Ask them to clench and then relax different parts of their body. Turn it into a game (trying to do this with ears is always fun). You can't feel stressed and relaxed at the same time. Make sure you are doing it too.

▶ Get into the habit of doing this when you both have time to relax, for example for ten minutes before they go to bed. If they practise regularly and enjoy the experience, it will be easier for them to do this when they feel tense.

C... Connect with their "coach"

Tips

▶ By asking children to focus on something positive, you change their frame of mind and perspective on a problem. Even if it is just for a few seconds, it will give them a little space.

- Connect with your child. Physical contact strengthens all connections. If appropriate, give them a cuddle or maybe a foot or shoulder massage.
- Help them to focus on an action inside their control that will help them take the first step towards a solution. By doing this, you are helping them to "respond" to a situation rather than just "react" and giving them practical tools and strategies to help them do something rather than just worry and do nothing. You're getting them "off the bench" and taking responsibility for their lives.

4. Help children manage their whole range of emotions in a positive way

Children who talk about their whole range of feelings, the positive and the challenging, are more likely to become more resilient. They learn to understand that all their emotions have an important part to play in their lives and how to manage them. They are much more likely to find solutions to problems through talking than reaching behavioural boiling point and lashing out physically or verbally.

Tips

- Reassure children that all their feelings are natural and normal. You have them too. They all have an important part to play in our emotional wellbeing and life. By helping them to take feelings in their stride and making it easy for them to chat about them now, they are much more likely to be doing this when they are teenagers. Get into good habits now.
- Focus on how you manage your feelings, especially the painful ones, and put some of the tools and techniques into practise yourself. If you talk about feeling stressed and do nothing about it, you feel more stressed.
- Show children that you are working at managing this in a positive and practical way and they will follow your example. You can try some visualisation and relaxation techniques together – and have fun doing it.

5. Be clear about your "success ethos" and focus on children's ACE (Attitude, Commitment and Effort)

It's common for children to believe that parents and teachers judge their success according to grades, getting into top sets, making the school team, etc. They think these are the most important measures of success and are a measure of their value as a person.

Tips

- Talk about what you all think. What is your family or class "success ethos" and how do you communicate this to your children? Involve them in creating that ethos so that they have ownership.

Perhaps success means taking responsibility, living your values, trying your hardest, having a go, doing what you believe is right or treating other people well and making a difference in the world. Decide what is important for all of you.

▶ Think ACE and recognise Attitude, Commitment and Effort. Focus more on the process than the product, more on the approach than the result. This will encourage children to become more resilient, to welcome challenges and to grow stronger through them. It helps them to avoid developing "perfectionist" tendencies. Remember personal best and perfection are very different things.

▶ Catch children "red-handed" being "successful." Give them specific, evidence-based feedback about the personal value, strength, skill or quality that they are demonstrating. Describe what you see. This information is filed on their personal memory sticks and helps to strengthen resilience and self-belief. You could, for example, create a "success" wall filled with all sorts of examples from home, from the classroom, in the playground, online, playing sport or drawing or performing, with friends and family.

6. Challenge self-limiting beliefs and quieten a child's inner critic with specific, evidence-based feedback

Self-limiting beliefs can be established at a very early age so it is helpful to start working on them as soon as you can. By using specific, evidence-based feedback, you are challenging powerful, negative self-limiting beliefs. Just like adults, children will often focus on the negative more than the positive.

Tips

▶ A child's brain is very different from an adult's brain so step into their shoes and see the world through their eyes. This will help you to understand what they are struggling with and be in the best place to help them manage this positively. Their resilient and confident self is developing, and you can really help them with this.

▶ Help children to examine the evidence, to listen to their inner coach. When they say, for example, "I am rubbish at maths and will never learn my 8 times table," draw a confidence cloud and fill it with all the times tables they do know.

- Now put a post-it with "8 times table" written on it just outside the cloud. Remember the value of the word "**yet**." "You don't know your 8 times table **yet**" or "You can't swim a length **yet**." It re-frames a task or activity for a child and creates the possibility that they will be able to do it at some point in the future.
- You can use a confidence cloud for any area of your child's life.

7. Put children in the driving seat with choice and responsibility

Use visualisation techniques – like Arty's – to help children talk about how they are feeling and to think about some of their worries in a different way.

There will always be things that happen outside their control, but there will always be things they can do themselves to help them feel more in control. Put them in the driving seat and help them to take responsibility for their lives, rather than feeling helpless because life is happening to them and is outside their control.

Tips

- Encourage children to find their own solutions. Children are very creative and have active imaginations. If they come up with their own ideas about solving problems, they are much more likely to make them work.
- If it works, do it again. If it doesn't, do something differently.
- If your child struggles to do their homework, involve them in scheduling it. Give them some choice. If, for example, they must do maths and English, ask them which one they want to do first and which one second. You may think it is good to do the one they struggle with first, then they can relax with the one they feel more confident in. But they may think the opposite and prefer to start with the one they enjoy more. They are going to do them both anyway, but this gives them responsibility in the scheduling. Their attention span is limited, so make sure you give them an energy break between subjects.

8. Build on strengths to weaken weaknesses – make connections

A child may be very may be very positive and resilient on a sports pitch or in an art class or performing in a play, but much less so in the classroom. It is very natural to focus on the areas where they feel least resilient because we want to boost their confidence in that area.

- ▶ Focus instead on the areas where they feel most resilient and focus on the skills, strengths and qualities they do have – it will strengthen confidence and resilience and help them to rise to challenges. By shining the light on those parts of their lives where they feel most resilient, we can help boost their resilience and "can-do" attitude across the board.
- ▶ Think about an area where your child demonstrates resilience and problem-solving abilities. You may, for example, talk to them about how they manage the pressures and challenges in sport or playing an instrument, or tackling a tricky friendship issue or managing a younger sibling.
- ▶ Be specific about what they do and help them to understand that these skills, qualities and strengths can be used in other areas of their life too. Help them to make their own connections.

9. Press the "pause" button and build reflection skills

Encourage children to reflect on what is going on in their world, to press the "pause" button and see how looking at what is happening can help them in the future.

Tips

- ▶ Boost reflection skills as much as you can – about what's happening in the classroom, in the playground and at home. If it works, do it again. If it doesn't, do something differently.
- ▶ Get into the habit of asking children "open" questions that help them to explore ideas and feelings rather than "closed" questions with a "yes" or "no" answer.
  - ▷ What worked? How can you build on it?
  - ▷ What have you learned from doing it?
  - ▷ What could you do differently next time?
- ▶ Encourage them to celebrate "failure" or things not going as planned as learning opportunities. Make sure you do too.

10. Think "connection" not "perfection" and "live in the moment"

You can't be 100% Mum, Dad or carer all the time – but you can be 100% some of the time. Those 100% times are vital. It is the times when you and your child are most relaxed and having fun that they are most likely to open up to you and reveal how they are feeling. You can tune in to what is really going on in their lives. This takes organising so call in your support networks and make it happen.

Spend time with children learning to "live in the moment." Children and adults who can do this are much more likely to be less anxious and more relaxed, positive, energised and optimistic. If you are thinking about what has happened in the past or may happen in the future, you cannot fully enjoy the present. Having fun with children helps them feel valued and secure. It turbo-boosts their resilience.

Tips

- Make a fun "to-do" list. Think of all the great things you would enjoy doing together. Or put each idea onto a piece of paper, pop them in a fun jar and take one out when you have some time to have fun together. Put them in the diary with a specific date and time, and make them happen.
- Go swimming, for a bike ride or camping.
- All have a go at a new, physical challenge – like ice skating or climbing.
- Read one of their favourite books in the dark with a torch or in an unusual location.
- Cook a meal together. Give it a theme – Indian, Mexican, Italian, Spanish or Chinese. Put on some music to get you in the mood and have fun creating dishes and eating them.
- Play a card game or board game or charades or sardines.
- Ask your child to teach you how to do something that they are better at than you.
- Have a family or class film afternoon or night (with no mobile phones, of course!).
- Take a picture of your family fun or class time. Print it out. Put it in a frame or on the fridge or on the wall. Surround yourselves with visual reminders of what being a family or class really means.